Disney's THE LION KING

Adapted by Justine Korman

Illustrated by Don Williams and H. R. Russell

A GOLDEN BOOK • NEW YORK
Western Publishing Company, Inc., Racine, Wisconsin 53404

From the smallest ant to the largest elephant, every living thing has a place in the great circle of life. Mufasa's place was king of the lions. Sarabi was the queen. And their newborn cub, Simba, would one day take his father's place as the Lion King.

But on this day little Simba rested in the hands of the wise baboon Rafiki, who sprinkled the cub with dust and welcomed the future king to the great circle of life. The elephants trumpeted, the wildebeests cheered, and the giraffes stamped their hooves for joy.

Mufasa's brother, Scar, did not attend the ceremony. He was not happy that Simba was next in line to rule the Pride Lands. Scar had always wanted to be king himself.

Time passed, and Simba grew. Early one morning Mufasa took him to the top of Pride Rock. "Simba, look," he said. "Everything the light touches is our kingdom."

"Wow!" the young lion said. Then he asked, "What about the shadowy place?"

"That's beyond our borders. You must never go there, Simba!" warned Mufasa.

Later Simba found Scar sunning on a rock. Simba proudly told his uncle, "Someday I'm gonna rule the whole kingdom! Well . . . everything except the shadowy place. My father said I can't go there."

"He's absolutely right," Scar slyly agreed. "An elephant graveyard is no place for a young prince. Only the bravest lions go there."

As Scar knew, Simba would want to prove that he was brave. So he said nothing as Simba hurried off to find his friend Nala and ask her to explore the mysterious Shadow Lands with him.

When the friends arrived at the Shadow Lands, they discovered an eerie place filled with elephant bones and spurts of steam.

"It's so creepy," whispered Nala excitedly.

"C'mon!" said Simba. "Let's check it out."

Zazu, the king's minister, had been looking for the cubs. When he caught up with them, he warned, "We are too far from the Pride Lands. It is dangerous!"

But Simba only said, "I walk on the wild side! I laugh in the face of danger! Ha-ha-ha!"

"Hee-hee-hee-hee-hee!" The strange laughter belonged to three hideous hyenas—Banzai, Shenzi, and Ed—who slinked out from an elephant skull.

When Zazu told the hyenas he was Mufasa's minister, they realized that Simba was the future king. "Look, boys! A king fit for a meal," Banzai snickered.

The hyenas chased Simba and Nala until the cubs were trapped.

Suddenly a thunderous RRRROARRRR! rattled rocks and bones. It was the roar of Mufasa, the Lion King! The frightened hyenas ran away.

That evening Mufasa had a talk with Simba.

"I was just trying to be brave like you," protested Simba.

Mufasa shook his head. "Being brave doesn't mean you look for trouble," he replied.

"Dad," Simba said suddenly, "we'll always be together, right?"

Mufasa gazed up at the sparkling heavens. "The great kings of the past look down on us from those stars," he said. "Whenever you feel alone, remember those kings will always be there to guide you. And so will I."

Scar was angry with the hyenas for letting Simba survive, but he made a bargain with them. If they helped make him king, they could have the run of the Pride Lands.

So Scar brought Simba to a vast gorge and promised the cub a wonderful surprise if he would wait on a certain rock. Then Scar signaled the hyenas.

The surprise turned out to be a stampeding herd of wildebeests, with the hyenas urging the herd on. The earth trembled, and dust choked the air as the wildebeests headed straight for Simba. He sought safety in a tree, but the branch he was on bent under his weight.

Suddenly Simba felt Mufasa grab him and carry him to a rocky ledge. Then through the thick, swirling dust, Simba saw his father disappear under the thundering herd.

Later Scar found Simba at the foot of a cliff, sobbing beside the lifeless body of his father.

Scar convinced the young cub that it was his fault the Lion King had died. Simba did not know that it was Scar who had pushed Mufasa to his death. Then Scar advised Simba to run away and never return.

Scar watched as Simba fled. Then he sent his hyenas to kill the cub. But the hyenas stopped when they reached a thorny thicket. "He'll never survive," they reasoned. So they returned to Pride Rock—and their new king, Scar.

Scar told the pride that there had been a terrible accident. Then he introduced the hyenas.

As Scar took control of the Pride Lands, Simba ran until he collapsed. Had it not been for two curious creatures—Timon the meerkat and Pumbaa, the fat, friendly warthog—Simba would surely have died.

Timon and Pumbaa took the cub to their jungle home and taught him how to live by *hakuna matata,* which meant "no worries." They also taught Simba to eat all kinds of insects.

Simba tried to put the past behind him. But on one clear night, the stars reminded him of the old kings and his father, Mufasa.

One day as a lioness chased Pumbaa, Simba rushed to protect his friend. The lioness flipped Simba onto his back—just the way Nala used to!

"Nala!" he cried.

"Simba?" the lioness said. "I thought you were dead." The friends embraced. Then Nala told Simba the sad story of the Pride Lands. Under cruel King Scar the land had become barren and the animals were starving.

But Simba refused to return and take his place as the Lion King. In his heart, he did not feel worthy.

That night wise old Rafiki found Simba alone.

"Who are you?" Simba asked.

"The question is, who are *you*?" asked Rafiki.

"I'm not sure anymore," Simba confessed.

"You're Mufasa's boy," the baboon declared. He led Simba to a small pool and said, "You see, he lives in you."

As Simba stared, he saw his father's face in the water. Then he heard his father's voice, and he looked up at the stars.

"Simba, look inside yourself," Mufasa commanded. "You are my son and the one true king. You must take your place in the circle of life."

So Simba set out to confront the false king.

Finally Pride Rock rose up out of a dry, empty plain. Hyenas were everywhere.

"I've come back to take my place as king," Simba announced to Scar. "Step down."

"Never!" snarled Scar, forcing Simba to the edge of Pride Rock. Then he told Simba the truth. "Here's a little secret. *I* killed your father. Too bad he isn't here to save you now."

Simba's heart filled with rage when he heard his uncle's words. He leaped on Scar—and the fight began!

Simba's friends had followed him back to Pride Rock. Nala led the other lionesses against the hyenas. Timon and Pumbaa joined the fray, and the hyenas were soon defeated.

Now Scar was the one on the edge of Pride Rock. He whimpered, "Please! Have pity on me."

"Run away, Scar," said Simba. "Run away and never return."

But when Simba turned his back, Scar attacked! Quick as lightning, Simba used Nala's trick flip to send Scar flying over the cliff to his death.

So Scar's evil reign ended, and Simba took his rightful place as the Lion King. In time, King Simba and Queen Nala had a cub of their own. From the smallest ant to the largest elephant, the beasts came from near and far to Pride Rock.

There the son of Simba rested in the hands of the wise baboon Rafiki, who sprinkled the cub with dust and welcomed the future king to the great circle of life which never ends.